No Ordinary Bones

By Julie Emch

AuthorHouse™
1663 Liberty Drive
Bloomington, IN 47403
www.authorhouse.com
Phone: 1-800-839-8640

Published by AuthorHouse 03/15/2013

ISBN: 978-1-4817-1557-7 (sc)
*   978-1-4817-1558-4 (e)*

Library of Congress Control Number: 2013902654

One bright, sunny day, Luke grabbed his science kit, called to J'amy and headed into the woods looking for adventure.

"Today is going to be one we will always remember," said Luke. "I feel it! Something very exciting will happen. We are going to make a great discovery. Probably be written up in one of those science magazines Dad reads. Who knows? We may even be rich and famous after today!"

"What do you think we will find?" asked J'amy, catching some of Luke's excitement.

"That's the best part," answered Luke, "not knowing until we find it!"

The two friends walked and walked. Just when they were starting to feel discouraged, like maybe they would find nothing, J'amy suddenly smelled something. "Over this way!" she called to Luke. "I smell something by this tree!"

Luke knelt down to get a better look. "It's bones! Wow! It's bones! This is better than I imagined! Now we can dig them up, take them back home and look at them under the microscope! We can use science to figure out what kind of an animal this was! Then we can use the forensic evidence to determine how it died!"

"Wait," asked J'amy a little nervously. "How do we know it's safe? How do we know it wasn't a ferocious animal?"

"We won't know until we dig the bones up and study them," answered Luke.

He started digging and pulling at the bones. "These bones are really stuck," he said. Then added excitedly, "There seems to be a whole skeleton here! This is so great! It's not very big. I think it must have been a mouse. Of course, we won't know for sure until we get them under the microscope."

"Oh, a mouse! Is that all? Good. Mice are cute little things. Not ferocious at all," said J'amy feeling relieved.

Luke dug and dug and pulled and pulled at the bones. "This skeleton is really buried in here! It must be bigger than I thought. It looks like a bird."

J'amy looked confused. "A bird? Are you sure? I thought you said it was a mouse. If it's a bird, that's ok. They can be fun to chase, and they sing. I like birds!"

Luke dug and dug and pulled and pulled at the bones. "These bones are buried really deep. It can't just be a bird! I really think this animal was a squirrel! Yea, a squirrel! Squirrel bones!" Luke shouted happily.

"A squirrel! Wow! I love to chase squirrels! That's probably my favorite animal!! I thought this was going to be scary, but a squirrel's not ferocious at all. This is exciting!" yelled J'amy.

Luke dug and dug and pulled and pulled at the bones. Then he shouted, "This skeleton is huge! It HAS to be a fox. Can you imagine? We found a fox skeleton!"

"What?!" screamed J'amy. "A fox? Are you kidding me? We can't deal with a fox! They're about my size, they have sharp teeth, and they ARE ferocious! Also, they are smarter than me! I can't protect you from a fox."

Luke dug and dug and pulled and pulled at the bones. "Wow, I can't believe how hard it is to get these bones loose. They are really buried deep, and they are big enough to be a wolf," he said.

"Did you say wolf?" whispered J'amy. "Wolf? Wolves are big and they don't mind eating dogs. And, they run in packs. Where there is one, there are many. I don't stand a chance against a ferocious wolf. Maybe we should forget about this and head home now."

Luke dug and dug and pulled and pulled at the bones. "These bones are too big to be just a wolf. They have to be a bear! I've never seen a real, live bear in these woods. Have you? I'm excited! Aren't you excited?" asked Luke.

"B-b-b-b-bear?... Excited isn't exactly the word I would use," J'amy answered with a quiver in her voice. "Nervous, scared, frightened, terrified..."

Luke dug and dug and pulled and pulled at the bones. "J'amy! J'amy!" he yelled. "This is awesome! We have discovered the skeleton of a woolly mammoth! I watched a show about them on the history channel! It showed people finding mammoth skeletons frozen in the arctic. They looked just like this! I wasn't sure they lived in these parts, but now we have proof! We have our very own skeleton. We can sell it to a museum. We will be rich!"

"Who cares about fame and fortune," cried J'amy. "I am afraid of woolly mammoths. They are HUGE! Do they eat dogs?"

Luke dug and dug and pulled and pulled at the bones. "J'amy, you're not going to believe this! These bones must have belonged to a dinosaur! I'm sure of it! They are THAT gigantic! If I had to take a guess, I would say it was a triceratops or a T-rex! Yea, that has to be it! A tyrannosaurus rex! You remember; we saw them on the science channel and in that movie that gave me nightmares!"

J'amy hid her face under her paws, whimpering, too frightened to talk.

Luke dug and dug and pulled and pulled at the bones until finally they were all free. He looked at his collection and started laughing. "J'amy, look! I was right all along! A MOUSE skeleton! I knew it! Let's call him Fred! He looks like a Fred. I think that is a good name for a mouse. We need to get these home and take a closer look. We have all the forensic evidence we need. Let's find out how Fred died."

"Oh, good!" said J'amy feeling relieved. "I like a cute, little, non-ferocious mouse skeleton much better than a dinosaur/mammoth/bear/wolf/fox/squirrel/bird."

As they walked home, J'amy started feeling better, but something was still bothering her. "Luke," she asked, "aren't you afraid you'll have nightmares tonight? I mean...I know I will. You really had me going with all that talk of bears and dinosaurs."

"Oh, no," answered Luke. "It's only a little mouse skeleton. It takes a lot more than that to give ME bad dreams."

While Luke got ready for bed, he kept thinking about the exciting day he and J'amy had. "This was the best day ever!" he said. "Tomorrow we will use the evidence to solve the mystery of Fred's death!" But J'amy was still worried about the dreams. Luke smiled at her, "You should be tough like me. I'll sleep like a baby."

"I'll try not to wake you up when I dream about being eaten by a t-rex," J'amy told him, and they both drifted off to sleep.

This book is based on a story my son, Luke, told us one day when we were in the car on our way from Green Bay, Wisconsin to Great Lakes, Illinois where he was learning to be a corpsman in the Navy. A corpsman is trained in the Navy and then serves with either the Navy or the Marines. Their job is to take care of the wounded or sick.

Luke had us in stitches we were laughing so hard, as he told us the story of finding and digging bones in the woods behind our home. I wanted to share a piece of that story with you, although I don't tell it as well as he.

Luke was very proud of being a corpsman. He wanted to help keep the marines who were fighting for our country safe. Luke served in the Iraqi war with a group of EOD marines. EOD stands for explosive ordinance disposal. These are the marines who find and disarm bombs (IED's) to keep the area safe for the other soldiers and marines. Luke was very good at taking care of his marines and saved many lives. Unfortunately, he was killed by one of these bombs on March 2, 2007.

Luke was smart, funny, brave, and compassionate. I miss him and hope sharing this small part of his life with you will help his memory to live on.

CPSIA information can be obtained
at www.ICGtesting.com
Printed in the USA
LVIC060527020513
331892LV00002B

9 7 8 1 4 8 1 7 1 5 5 7 7